A Peek Inside

Now, just a good-for-nothing minute. He did *not* remember Virginia Abbott, in all her prattling on about her Halloween party, asking his permission to tell ghost stories *in his house!*

Without one lost second, the Erickson delinquent turned the doorknob to the dining room and led his accomplices inside.

The miscreants had entered his house! Uninvited. Unwanted.

And, if their story was accurate, any number of young ladies were already inside.

Gus shook off the aggravation and drew deeply of cold, autumn air. Throw them out? Lock them up? Make trouble for the perpetrators?

They wanted ghost stories in a haunted house? He grinned. He'd give them a haunting they'd never forget.

Praise For

5 Goodreads Stars: "Just finished reading this short story by Kristin Holt. Loved it!! Great addition her Mountain Home collection! love her books."

~ Toni, Goodreads Reviewer (11-3-17)

5 Goodreads Stars: "Just finished The Witching Eve by Kristin Holt. It was a charming short story the makes me want to read the books about the same characters so that I can learn more about them."

~ Pam Evans, Goodreads Reviewer (11-1-17)

The Witching Eve

A *Holidays in Mountain Home*
Short Story
Title 7

by

USA TODAY Bestselling Author

KRISTIN HOLT

All titles stand alone and may be enjoyed in any order.

Copy Edit by **RVP The Man Editing**:
https://RVPTheManEditing.weebly.com/
Image copyright © Jakkapan Jabjainai / Freepik subscription license
Series cover design copyright © 2018 by Kelli Ann at Inspire Creative Services:
www.InspireCreativeServices.com
ebook and paperback cover design by Kristin Holt
ebook and paperback interior design by Kristin Holt

A Holidays in Mountain Home
SHORT STORY

Halloween, 1900
Mountain Home, Colorado

Between MAYBE THIS CHRISTMAS and THE MARSHAL'S SURRENDER...

Blame it on the moon.

Before U.S. Marshal-turned-Sheriff August "Gus" Rose fell in love with Noelle Finlay in THE MARSHAL'S SURRENDER, their paths crossed on Halloween. That full-moon night might have begun like so many All Hallows Eves in Noelle's life, but quick as a wink, the parlor games take a turn for the worse. What better place to tell ghost stories than in a haunted house?

"It's all fun and games until somebody gets hurt."

What is lawman Gus to do when the trouble-seeking girls use his house— complete with cobwebs and shadows— for their ghost stories? Will he arrive in time to save Noelle?

Though mildly spooky, this tale contains elements of sweet romance, clean (language), and *mild* elements of (Halloween) violence.

Learn much more about the
Holidays in Mountain Home Series here:

www.KristinHolt.com/holidays-in-mountain-home-series

(case is irrelevant, but it's critical to spell Kristin with two i's and no e's; "Kristin is e-free")

HOLIDAYS IN MOUNTAIN HOME

Series

as of September 2018
(with many more titles to follow):
In Chronological Order:

Courting Miss Cartwright (Rocky & Felicity),
1879
Book #5, Founder's Day NOVELLA

This Noelle (Phil & Caroline), **1881**
Prequel: Book #0.5, Christmas NOVELLA

The Gunsmith's Bride (Morgan & Elizabeth),
1885
Book #6, Independence Day NOVELLA

Unmistakably Yours (Hank & Jane, Oscar &
Ina), **1887**
Book #8, Thanksgiving NOVEL

Home for Christmas (Hunter & Miranda), **1898**
Book #1, Christmas NOVELLA

Maybe This Christmas (Luke & Effie), **1899**
Book #2, <u>Christmas</u> NOVELLA

The Witching Eve (Gus & Noelle), **1900**
Title #7, <u>Halloween</u> SHORT STORY

The Marshal's Surrender (Gus & Noelle), **1900**
Book #3, <u>Christmas</u> NOVEL

The Drifter's Proposal (Malloy & Adaline), **1900**
Book #4, <u>Christmas</u> NOVELLA

Find links to website pages dedicated to each
book on the Holidays in Mountain Home Series
Page:
www.KristinHolt.com/holidays-in-
mountain-home-series

*(case is irrelevant, but it's critical to spell Kristin
with two i's and no e's; "Kristin is e-free")*

THE WITCH'S COMPLAINT

Oh, yes, of course, it's all our fault!
The milk is sour, the sugar's salt!
The gate is stolen from the fence—
It's up a pole full twelve blocks hence!
A rope is stretched across the walk—
Of course! Just go ahead and talk!
All of the tricks that you have seen
You lay on us on Hallowe'en!

It is the night of all the year
That we have chosen for good cheer.
We race on broomsticks through the air
And witches' celebrations share.
We have a lot of harmless sport—
It isn't fair that you report
That we are out on mischief bent.
Witches for that are never meant.

We see the harm you children do—
It makes us angry through and through.
What right have you to spoil our fun
With all the naughty things you've done?
What is the sense in tipping wood
And ruining things, whole and good?
You might at least stay safe at home
This night we witches choose to roam!

~ *The Jolly Hallowe'en* Book by Dorothy M. Shipman and Others, Copyright 1900 by The Willis N. Bugbee Co., p. 16. Now in <u>Public Domain</u>.

All Hallows Eve, 1900
Mountain Home, Colorado

Lawmen everywhere swore the moon did more than pull the tides. A new moon, with her cloak of darkness, tempted the worst of men to burgle, arson, and attack.

Laws of nature no longer held true, once the moon waxed full.

Lunar light provoked lunacy, everywhere. Didn't matter if those folks wore fine suits of clothes or durable clothes of the laborer.

So far, no hint of mayhem. No roaming

gangs bent on pranking.

He tucked a smoke between his teeth and reached for a match before he'd realized he wanted another. Not that he was nervous. He'd handle what came. The Hartford police force had been out in numbers each hallow's eve.

In this small town, one badge was enough to patrol the streets. Folks outside town— ranchers, miners, farmers— were more than accustomed to protecting their own while looking out for their neighbors.

This might be August Rose's first Halloween as Mountain Home's sheriff, but he'd lawed a long while with the U.S. Marshals.

Beneath his heel, Gus crushed the embers from his smoke, then rested the sole of one boot against the jailhouse wall. He leaned against its rough planks. Chilly wind scuttled past, carrying familiar odors of kitchen woodsmoke and burned stubble from fields put to bed 'til spring.

He scanned the street, honed every sense, discarded normal noises of the town buttoning up for the night. Wagons rattled down the street, drawn by horses heading for the barn and a bucket of oats. Shopkeepers waved, calling their goodnight in parting.

One familiar mare trotted opposite that natural flow toward home and hearth. Should've known Miss Noelle Finlay would head into town just as twilight gave way to night.

Virginia Abbott had prattled on and on about her annual Halloween party— secret guest list, ghost stories, and games of fortune. She'd chattered a good half hour 'bout glimpsing his visage in a mirror. Drivel he'd barely heard, but he'd heard enough to know Noelle's name was on that guest list.

Noelle, four or five miles from home, between sunset and moon-rise, caused no worry. Unlike others her age, she had a level head. She'd probably overnight at her brother's.

That brother had caused Gus more than passing trouble. Ten months and counting, and the memory of losing Effie to Luke Finlay still pierced his hide with savage claws.

Personal pain or not, he had a job to do.

She drew nearer, the reins too tight for a woman at perfect ease.

He swept his Stetson from his head in acknowledgment. Admiration. And respect.

He'd noticed her about town, delivering orders, attending church. Unlike other women her age, she never spoke ill of others. Two months back, she'd helped two old women move their chairs closer to the celebration. Her smile had roped him, sure as a lariat slipped over a steer's horns. He'd asked her to dance, and enjoyed it so much, he'd returned for seconds.

Now, all too soon, yet not quick enough, she and Buttercup passed by.

He stuffed his hat back in place, drew hard on his cigarette, and forced the smoke to escape through his nostrils. He glared at the brilliant light of the full moon, rising from her slumber behind the Rockies. "Luna, simmer down, will you? This town don't need your kind of crazy."

He took stock of himself, talking to a hunk of rock orbiting the earth. The lunacy had started. Moon rise, not three minutes past, had struck him first. "*I* don't need your kind of crazy."

At seven o'clock, Noelle Finlay arrived at Belle Talmadge's home in town. Supper would be followed by games at Virginia Abbott's residence.

She would've replied with regrets, but the event gave her an excuse to stay overnight in town with her brother, Luke, and his wife, Effie. Which, in turn, doubled— no, *quintupled*— the possibility of glimpsing Sheriff August Rose.

He'd snagged her attention the moment he'd arrived in Mountain Home. Evidently, he'd enthralled Virginia and Belle. The two played tug of war, Gus caught between, ever since.

In a cacophony of giggles and rose-scented

hugs, the twelve long-standing guests met in the dining room and took their usual places.

As traditional this ghostly night of the year, all gas lamps had been banned, and two dozen candles, spread among three candelabra, lit the table, glanced off china and crystal and silver. Autumn spices of cinnamon, cloves, and nutmeg simmered together with lemons in a potpourri of fragrance. Dry cornstalks stood as sentinels in the corners, tied with torn strips of flannel in seasonal colors of red, orange, and gold.

Even the spooky menu, with indecipherable names, remained unchanged.

Tradition was all well and good, but had Virginia and Belle no imagination?

Mrs. Talmadge set a dessert plate with a precisely cut square of cake before each guest. The fortune-telling emblems baked within would be too easily seen within a layer cake.

"Ladies." Virginia giggled. "Our Halloween cake."

At last, something different! Last year's had been Devil's Food with luscious, whipped frosting. Tonight's carrot cake, with spices, chopped nuts, and raisins, tasted decadent.

At Noelle's left, Alice, who'd consumed very little during supper, poked the tines of her fork at precise, close intervals searching for hidden fortune. Evidently, Alice focused on a reducing diet. She'd gained a good deal of flesh since moving from farm to town.

Nearly everyone else chattered as they ate, exclaiming with joy and distress as they unearthed the trinkets baked within.

Anyone who believed in follies such as fortunes foretold by barmbrack deserved what they got.

"The ring!" Virginia Abbott squealed. "I found the wedding ring!" *Married within the year,* or so the charm promised.

Nearly everyone replied simultaneously.

"Already?"

"Lucky, lucky."

"No!"

"Again?" Belle's tone made it clear she found no joy in the idea of Virginia married.

The way Belle and Virginia bickered over whose turn it was to claim Gus, Belle no doubt feared she'd lose the man altogether.

Virginia's expression proclaimed she wanted the fortune-telling to prove true. No doubt, she hoped, to the handsome sheriff.

The thought of Gus wed to Virginia soured Noelle's stomach, though she most certainly did not believe in fortune telling. She stabbed her fork into frosting and cake. Two cream cheese-frosted bites later, her fork sounded upon metal.

Thimble? Coin? Button? Key? Must be. The tine hadn't struck wood. Or cloth.

Pauline whooped and held her fork aloft,

spearing the same brass thimble that had made its way through nearly everyone, one Halloween cake at a time. "Shall I break the news of my impending spinsterhood to James?"

Laughter and good-natured ribbing had Pauline trying the thimble on her ring finger. "I do believe I'll make a fine spinster, don't you?"

Hadn't Noelle heard that the sewing circle, a club involving the town's young ladies, an invitation she'd turned down (who had time for such frivolities?), had finished a quilt for Pauline's trousseau, only last month? Everyone knew Pauline and James intended to marry, come spring.

Noelle had consumed most of her cake, little bite by little bite, until only the morsels masking the foreign object remained.

"I have the button." Belle giggled, gleeful. "If I were masculine, I'd be a bachelor. Oh well, I see my fortune is all mixed up."

"A button?" Mary gestured for Belle to pass the item. "We've never had a button in the cake."

"It *is* a button."

Despite the mess of cake, Belle passed the button to her right, from guest to guest, at last coming to rest in Mary's palm. "Why did your mother put a button in the cake? All guests are girls. *Women*. No bachelors here."

"Mother didn't bake the cake. She took the tokens to Whipple's Bakery and placed the order."

If Adaline Whipple, the baker's daughter, had added a button to the recipe, what else might she have decided to throw in? Noelle peered closer, but in the flickering candlelight, the cake of many colors and textures revealed nothing.

At her right, Della leaned in better to see. "What do you have in yours, Noelle?"

Noelle slid her fork into the last bite with ease, and lifted it from the plate. "Nothing, I believe." Maybe she'd encountered a nut, earlier, or bit of shell.

"That's a shame."

Perhaps for those who enjoyed this diversion. She'd never been one to enjoy the traditional games on All Hallow's Eve. She'd long ago determined the only way to determine her future was to create it.

As Belle took stock of the prizes, and their winning ladies, pausing to exclaim over a second penny. "Two pennies?"

Chatter rose. Two pennies, one at the foot of the table and one near the head, were displayed on palms for all to see.

The last bite of cake melted on her tongue... leaving behind something hard. Circular. Flat.

Had she somehow missed another coin? Would this make her heiress to a purported fortune, along with Gertie and Ruby?

She rolled the object over and quickly noted its hollow center. A ring.

Her stomach, moments ago comfortably full, seemed suddenly quite empty.

Had Mrs. Talmadge provided Whipple Bakery with *two* rings? Or maybe Adaline Whipple hoped to add to the fun?

Lifting her napkin to her mouth, she blotted her lips and carefully slipped the object from her mouth.

There, indeed. A slim gold band. She immediately sought Kathleen's eyes across the table.

"You found a ring, too?" Kathleen bounded out of her chair, manners abandoned.

The All Hallow's Eve party seemed not so repetitious, after all.

If Noelle put an ounce of credence in foolish parlor games of fortunetelling, she'd be consumed by the prophecy of marriage, *for her*, within the year.

Tingling began in the vicinity of her stomach, lifting it to touch her heart. Gus had been quick to lift his hat when she'd passed him on the street not two hours ago.

He'd sought her out in the crowd on Founder's Day, asking her to dance with him. Not once, but twice.

Mrs. Talmadge paused between refilling two cups of coffee. She touched Noelle's shoulder. "You have the second ring, do you, my dear?"

"I do." Against her better judgment, Noelle held up the band. Smudged from the sugary treat, she was tempted to swish it off in her water goblet. Unlike Kathleen, she hadn't lost her senses.

"Indeed. With all twelve of you approaching marriageable age, it seemed prudent to tuck in at least two rings."

Ah, Mrs. Talmadge was the culprit. Halloween was the night for pranks.

"I'll be!" Virginia slid her chair back a few inches, cutting off all discussions. "I found the key."

She held the same little jewelry box key hidden in a decade of holiday cakes.

Noelle watched Virginia track her mother's progress, empty coffee pot in hand, as she left the dining room.

The moment the kitchen door swung closed, the little key clattered upon her empty dessert plate. She brandished a different key, much larger, too clean to suppose it had been within carrot cake. Too large, given the petite dessert squares.

A house key?

Virginia pressed a forefinger to her lips, urging silence.

"Ladies." Belle stood, drawing all into her

conspiratorial smile. "We're off now, to Virginia's home, for the evening's entertainment. Ghost stories and more games of fortune."

Seconds passed without anyone rising.

Alice met Noelle's gaze, then darted to the mutilated and untasted cake square upon her plate.

Foreboding stole through Noelle. Whatever lock that key fit, it would not be Virginia Abbott's door.

An hour past moon-rise, Luna's Pied Piper routine had led too many outside to do their worst. Gus had noted three different roving gangs of boys ranging from age six to twenty-six.

Until somebody crossed the line from harmless to destructive, he'd allow their fun. The witching eve was the one time each year when boys could be boys.

Let them blame the bizarre happenings on witches. The law knew better.

Yes, another lawman would stop the pranks immediately. The way he saw things, all three gangs were comprised of decent boys. Good thing Gus didn't need much sleep. He'd patrol 'til dawn, have a big cup of coffee or two, then round up the offenders.

He'd see to it they put everything back where they found it. Somehow, the boys would figure out how to lower Dr. Cheney's gate from the telegraph pole. The four Murphy boys had traded every last rocking chair from the boarding house front porch with those of every neighbor on the street. The gang of mature men had managed to hoist the new attorney's carriage into his neighbor's hayloft. Payment for some slight, Gus imagined, and probably well-deserved.

Off to his right, wood slid against wood... a window sash opened. One young head popped through, looked left, then right, then left again. Quick as a whistle, the youth bounded over the sill and pulled his brother through. The mites couldn't be more than six or seven years of age. The bigger of the two lowered the window, until barely room for child-sized fingers remained. Smart boy allowed for reentry. He'd sneaked out before.

Gus searched his memory for the family's name... Miller. Yes, Miller.

"If Dad notices we're gone," the little one whispered loud enough to wake the dead, "we're gonna get the belt."

The elder brother clamped a hand over the

rascal's mouth. "Then make sure he don't notice. Be quiet."

The boys scurried through the lot, keeping to the shadows. The moon's glow shone bright enough to see them, plain as day. Glancing neither left nor right, the pair trotted, a clear destination in mind.

Gus nearly grinned as the Miller pair slowed near the jailhouse. Without a prisoner, the building was locked up tight, not a single lamp lit. The guns were locked up too.

The older boy bypassed the jailhouse and headed straight for the impound lot. He shushed his brother, and threw a startled look over both shoulders. Good, Gus hadn't yet lost his knack for tracking without detection. In contrast, the boys needed prowling lessons.

The boys tested the lock and rattled the chain.

Five horses, impounded for various infractions— nibbling Mrs. Cheney's rosebushes, running amok and lunching on sacks of flour and oats in the backs of waiting buckboards— moseyed toward the boys. One whinnied just loud enough to block the boys' conversation.

None of those misbehaving, flea-bitten, bag-of-bones equines belonged to the Millers.

Huddled together, the pair managed to block Gus's view. His smile slipped. If the pair wanted in, they'd have scaled the fence....

The gate swung open.

The brats discharged the padlock. *Picking locks... in short pants?*

Gus rapidly tallied the lost revenue for the city as Old Campbell's cantankerous stallion led the way to freedom, two mares and two geldings close behind. He took three long strides toward the pair, ready to grab them by the ears when the second gang— men in their late teens and early twenties— trotted between buildings and rounded the corner. He recognized Victor Erickson, the young man whose rich father owned a ranch outside town, and caused his good mother far too much distress.

That one was up to no good.

"Yes, I'm sure." Erickson's voice?

"How do you know?" Muffled, unidentifiable.

"'Cause I saw him, trailing the old men bent on hiding Van Pletzen's new carriage."

Him. Gus. He'd tailed the *old men.*

"No, I mean," *puff, puff*— the shorter one couldn't run and keep his breath, "how you know," *puff, puff,* "he won't be home? I ain't keen," *gasp, gasp,* "on breaking in—"

"I told you. My sister has a key."

A break-in crossed the line. Key or no key.

Gus glanced back to the Millers, shutting the gate and returning the lock, as if the horses had managed to jump the impound corral fence, and quickly determined to follow Erickson's gang.

Gus could have growled upon discovering the boys' destination.

Every last one stood on *his* lawn, beside *his* door leading into *his* dining room. A door he never used because he never occupied that part of the far-too-large-for-one-man house.

"I hear he lives in the kitchen." Unidentifiable.

Why, when he grabbed that scoundrel—

"Why does an old bachelor need Abbott's mansion?"

"*Quiet!*"

Gus fought to control his temper, to listen. Wind. Rustling leaves. Six or seven lads, a few with their chests working like billows. Full moonlight, and their positions, finally revealed their faces.

He could name two of the six. Enough to uncover the rest.

Seconds passed, then close to a full minute. Erickson must've decided they weren't observed— *lunacy!*— and rallied his troops. "My sister's at her friend's stupid Halloween party. Always used to be here, when Abbotts owned the place. They're coming here tonight to tell ghost stories, upstairs, in the abandoned, haunted, cobweb-strewn bedrooms."

Now, just a good-for-nothing minute. He

did *not* remember Virginia Abbott, in all her prattling on about her Halloween party, asking his permission to tell ghost stories *in his house!*

Without one lost second, the Erickson delinquent turned the doorknob to the dining room and led his accomplices inside.

The miscreants had entered his house! Uninvited. Unwanted.

And, if their story was accurate, any number of young ladies were already inside.

Gus shook off the aggravation and drew deeply of cold, autumn air. Throw them out? Lock them up? Make trouble for the perpetrators?

They wanted ghost stories in a haunted house? He grinned. He'd give them a haunting they'd never forget.

Noelle remembered the entirety of Virginia Abbott's former home, quite well. She'd not only attended yearly Halloween parties here, she'd visited upon occasion. As school girls, she and Virginia had been good friends. Now, she couldn't remember why she'd admired Virginia.

Or this house.

Following at the tail end of twelve girls traipsing up the dusty staircase, the air stale and close, cobwebs brushing past her face and giving her the willies, this house felt empty.

Hollow.

Unloved.

At the top of the stairs, a knot of girls had formed, huddled close to Virginia, whose single candle cast light to bounce upon the ceiling and long, eerie shadows across walls, floors, and gaping doorways.

Noelle shivered.

"Why is Sheriff Rose's house empty?" Ruby's voice sounded small in the vacant hallway.

"He refuses to live up here." Virginia turned and headed toward the Master bedroom.

So, the rumors were true. A strange ache settled behind Noelle's breastbone and throbbed in time with her heartbeat. That ache swelled... almost as if she understood Gus, felt his sadness, and his regret for what might have been.

No wonder he avoided the rooms meant for family.

The group passed by the Mistress's room, once inhabited by Mrs. Abbott. Would Gus still think of Effie, if he were to pass this door?

When the Abbotts had resided here, the house had been full of love and light. Now, the building had lost that sense of *home*.

Inside the Master bedchamber, the window gaped like an open maw, devoid of the velvet draperies that had once hung there. Moonlight streamed through dirty panes, the giant orb radiant in the night sky. Wisps of clouds crowded in, seeming to double in that moment.

As if darkness went hand-in-hand with ghost stories.

"Where does he live, if not here?" Mary huddled close to Ruby.

Noelle had heard rumors, that Gus confined himself to the maid's room, with space enough for a cot and wash bowl only, and the kitchen.

"In the kitchen and the maid's room." Virginia seemed confident. Certain.

Had Noelle *ever* heard anything so sad? A man engulfed in loneliness, distressed by rejection. Why did no one care about why he lived in two rooms, only?

Had Virginia heard rumors, or had she peered at him through the windows? Far too respectable to pay a call on Gus at home— though she had no such scruples about calling on him at the jail house— she must have spied.

The idea of Virginia peering through windows, watching Gus in his home, made her blood rush hot and fast.

Clueless, Virginia turned the doorknob. "That's why we're here. He won't be home for hours, not that he'd come up here. Can you imagine a *better* place for ghost stories?"

Noelle refused to remain silent. "We should not be here."

"So you've said." Virginia sounded too much like her mother. Bossy. Correct. Entitled. "Thrice. Are you scared?" Her voice adopted the sing-song way of speaking to babies. Or the simple-minded.

"This is not your home. Not any longer." Noelle folded her arms and glared past the glowing firelight of Virginia's candle.

"It was," Virginia stated in a tone that dared Noelle to argue. "And it will be, again, when Sheriff August Rose and I wed."

"That eventuality remains to be decided." Belle slipped her arm through Virginia's.

Why Belle had replied with calm, Noelle couldn't comprehend. Both girls were determined to win his affection. Telling ghost stories in the Master bedroom of his home, uninvited, seemed imprudent.

"Enough discussion. Form a circle, ladies." Belle motioned the others into position. "And join arms."

"Form a witch's circle?" Kathleen's voice echoed fright. She clung to Noelle's arm on one side, and Alice's on the other.

"No. I'm not going to tell you a *witch's* story, Kathleen. I'm here to tell *ghost* stories."

Noelle's ire rose. "Virginia, that was mean. Apologize to Kathleen."

Virginia smirked. "Kathleen, are you here to listen to ghost stories, or not?"

Kathleen lowered her gaze to the dusty floorboards. "I'm here to, um...listen." She swallowed, an audible click in her throat.

Noelle may have decided, on the lawn, in the dark, as Virginia drew the candle, matches, and key from her reticule, that she must come inside with the girls, ensure they did no damage to Gus's house, but that was *then*.

Much had changed in the recent past. Perhaps *she* had changed. "No, you're not."

"I'm not?" Kathleen blinked. Panic widened her eyes, showing white all about the soft brown irises.

Noelle squeezed Kathleen's hand where it lay in the crook of her own arm. "And neither am I. This party is finished."

Belle gasped, her eyes wide with disbelief. "How dare you?"

The candle flame flickered and jumped, as if someone had tried to blow it out, but from too great a distance.

"I dare," Noelle insisted, "because this is wrong. *You* are wrong to plan this... this..." She gestured at the room, Gus's house, their party in his home.

An inhuman screech sounded in tandem— Belle and Virginia united against a common enemy.

Noelle dragged Kathleen back a step, away from their hostesses turned attackers. "Go," she urged Kathleen, whose arm was still linked tightly with Alice's.

Several of the women scrambled behind

Noelle, heading toward the bedroom door.

The rustle of party dresses combined with the patter of feet.

Commotion on the stairs erupted in a flurry of voices, but Noelle's focus remained on the two witches glaring at her in twin fury.

With rage glowing by candlelight in her eyes, Virginia swept her thumb and forefinger over her tongue to wet them, then pinched the candle flame.

The faint sputter barely registered against the backdrop of thudding shoes on stair treads as darkness engulfed the room.

Gus followed the pack of men inside. They seemed to know, immediately, where the women would be, because they'd taken to the staircase without hesitation. Their boots made a racket on the bare treads.

Disjointed sounds indicated trouble.

Feminine gasps, little feet, a woman or two crying.

The ladies, it seemed, were coming down the stairs as fast as the men were headed up them. They collided somewhere in the middle.

Moonlight drenched the hallway through an upstairs window, giving partial view to the collision, but the bottom of the staircase, where

Gus stood, lay in full shadow.

Time for that promised haunting. Gus drew a deep breath and bellowed, "Who dares disturb my slumber?"

A dozen girls shrieked in panic.

The mass of humans struggled to move down the stairs, then seemed to think better of it and surged upward, fighting to put significant distance between the apparition— Gus— and themselves.

A knot of boys— how could he call them men?— elbowed their way past a few women visible in moonlight and onto the landing, jabbering like birds on a telegraph wire, shouting orders mixed with exclamations.

He couldn't be sure, in the commotion, but two of those boys might've shrieked in distress.

"Run!" an unidentified male voice cried.

Footsteps pounded, echoing in the empty rooms, bouncing off bare floors and high ceilings. Eventually, they'd find the servants' staircase on the opposite end of the hallway.

'Til then, Gus intended to have some fun. "Fee!" he bellowed. "Fi. Fo." Laughter erupted as the boys shouted and the girls squealed.

In the melee, Virginia's shrieks demanded her horde hold their ground. "It's only Gus!"

So, the silly twit recognized his voice, had she? Given her actions this night, he was justified in pranking her in return, right?

Some of the men on the staircase gave up shoving the knot of girls higher on the staircase, thus ensuring their escape, and turned downward.

Gus leapt off the staircase in time to avoid being trampled, cupped his hands about his mouth, and bellowed up the staircase. "Virginia Abbott!"

The floor vibrated with the stampede toward the door. A masculine *umph* sounded as one of the men crashed down the last few steps.

Gus tried to hold in his laughter. He tried, and failed. He laughed as he hadn't laughed in a long while. Even as the demons who'd broken into his home reached a full head of steam and chugged toward egress.

Silk dresses, whispering like autumn wind, and female voices chattering like clattering wheels upon iron rails made up the middle of the train. One decidedly feminine figure brought up the rear, her skirts hiked up in two fists, moving fast.

"Virginia!" Gus yelled once more, unsure if she'd been one to flee or if she remained in his haunted house.

The dining room door, giving way into the garden, slammed shut.

Gus chuckled. What fun! He ought to spook interlopers more often.

Footfalls in the bedrooms upstairs sounded

too light and tentative to be the male ringleaders, cocky in their plan to follow the ladies inside. Not so sure any more, were they?

"Sh-Sh-Sheriff?"

"That you, Miss Virginia?"

"Um....no?"

He didn't recognize the feminine voice. "You up there alone?"

"Um...I don't know. *Oh*." A thud, followed by sobs.

"Stay right there," he urged, even as he ran for the oil lamp on his kitchen table.

Seconds later, he'd lit and carried the lamp high, peering through the wavering shadows at the top of the stairs.

He thought he glimpsed a person or two huddled behind the banister in the hall above.

"I'm coming up," he called ahead, determined to avoid scaring a woman more than necessary. Unless that woman happened to be Virginia. She deserved another fright.

He took the stairs one at a time, when the lawman in him wanted to take them two or three at once.

"You ladies all right?"

Three of them huddled together on the dirty floor. Two of them had tears streaming down their cheeks. Somehow, he doubted these were tears of laughter.

The third one, unfortunately, lay quiet,

draped over the second one's lap.

Noelle.

Eyes closed, posture boneless, and blood pooled at the corner of her mouth.

Fear spiked, spurring his heart into a gallop. No, no!

He touched the pulse at her throat, relieved at the steady rhythm of her heart.

He pulled the handkerchief out of his pocket and dabbed blood from Noelle's lower lip.

The two conscious women cried harder.

"I didn't see her," the first insisted, her words soggy with tears. "I tripped over her."

The second one, plump and wide-eyed, repeated the same phrase over and over, but so distorted were her words, so unintelligible, he couldn't understand.

He'd been a fool. Some lawman he was, allowing this prank to turn from fun to terror in his own home. He'd been the one to touch match to fuse, with his ridiculous prank, and spooked the crowd.

Noelle had paid the price.

He had to find Doc Cheney, but that would mean leaving Noelle unconscious with two hysterical women. Without apology, Gus methodically searched Noelle's limbs for breaks. No way to tell if she had broken ribs. He touched her waist, relieved to find a rigid corset beneath his fingers. The constraint would have protected her spine and internal organs.

"Let me take her." He lifted Noelle into his arms and stood, prepared to carry her downstairs to the much warmer kitchen, perhaps to his cot, and there instruct the two women to wait with her while he went in search of Doc.

Despite his panic, the scent of Noelle's soap and the softness of her slight weight invaded his senses. Awareness shoved aside fear, awareness of a woman, as a woman, for the first time since Effie.

Odd. And wonderful. And terrifying.

Halfway down the stairs, the plump woman's cries suddenly registered.

He whirled, finding her on his heels. "What did you say?"

She swiped tears from her plump cheeks. "Ginnyhurther," *gasp*, "Ginnyhurther, Ginnyhurther."

"Ginny? Virginia." His blood rushed hot and fast through his veins. He'd choke the life out of Virginia Abbott.

The woman nodded. Relief washed through her, and in the precarious moment, on the stairs, he feared she'd faint, and tumble to the bottom. His arms were full of one woman; he couldn't protect another.

He speared the second with a hard glare, jerking his head toward the plump one. "Grab her. Sit on the stairs and slide down, one at a time if you have to."

The women clung to each other, following behind as he carried Noelle, unconscious and bleeding, toward bed.

A week later, once all the post-Halloween nonsense was cleared up, when Gus could put off his visit to the Finlay ranch no longer, he rode out to pay Noelle a call. He walked Beau every step of the four miles, though the gelding wanted his head and to run.

Gus might not need much sleep, but over the past week, since the lunacy of the full moon, he'd managed only a few hours here and a few hours there. He kept seeing Noelle unconscious and vulnerable on his upstairs hall floor.

In his dreams, Noelle was alone, without protection.

In some particularly disturbing nightmares,

Virginia did far more than strike Noelle with a fist.

Maybe, once he paid this call— though he hated visiting the Finlay place, and Luke Finlay was still his nemesis and likely always would be— the dreams would leave him be.

Mrs. Finlay greeted Gus at the front door and welcomed him warmly. "Come in, Sheriff. Noelle's in the kitchen."

He whacked his Stetson against his thigh until Mrs. Finlay took it from him, and demanded his coat for good measure.

"Ma'am, I won't be staying long enough to part with my coat. Or my hat."

She stood a little taller and wiggled her fingers with an unmistakable and unspoken *now, boy.*

Without his coat and hat, Gus found Noelle in the kitchen.

The room smelled of home. Freshly baked bread cooled on the table, the loaves resting on their sides. An utter mystery to him, but then, bread wasn't his specialty. He was a lawman, always had been, always would be.

And as a lawman, he'd failed to keep his town safe over the asinine Witching Eve. In all fairness, the town was fine. No structures had burned down. Every fence was back on its hinges and all bewitched property back where it belonged.

"Gus." She turned from the sink where she'd been washing dishes. The bruise on her jaw clobbered him all over again.

"I'm fine," she insisted.

Noelle was young, younger than Effie, too young for the likes of him. But to look into her eyes...

"I'm fine," she repeated.

How did she—

"You shouldn't play poker, Sheriff. Your every thought is plain as day on your face."

Not good. What had she seen? He didn't like the idea of this woman reading him so easily. Especially with his reaction to her out of sorts. All started with her injury, he supposed, and carrying her downstairs, rushing for the doctor, his gut tied in knots and worried sick.

He shifted his weight from one boot to the other.

Blame it on the full moon.

The blasted flickers of awareness that started that night wouldn't leave him be.

Blame it all, all the craziness, on that full moon.

He'd been completely dead inside, dead to the likes of every woman, since Effie. He preferred it that way. Closed off and unfeeling meant he couldn't hurt.

He cleared his throat, banished the unwelcome thoughts. "You doing all right?"

She touched her jaw carefully, with the tips of two fingers, where Virginia's right hook had connected.

He flinched.

"Barely hurts anymore. I don't remember anything after she doused the candle."

"That's probably best." He couldn't meet her eye. Did she remember his part in the tomfoolery?

The moment stretched, and he grew restless, desperate to return to town. First, he had things to say. "Miss Virginia Abbott stood before the judge this morning, for assaulting you."

"That's not necessary." She shook her head with vehemence, but appeared to think better of it. She winced. "I told you I didn't want to press charges."

"*I* pressed charges."

Noelle's eyes rounded. "Why?"

Evidently, Noelle thought little Virginia Abbott had a chance of leaving a mark on him. "She entered my house without permission. Brought all you ladies along with her, a flame in her hand, with intent to cause bedlam. That trouble culminated with her striking you."

Noelle grinned. "What did the judge say?"

"She's in loads of trouble."

"Oh?" Her eyes sparkled, as if she thought Virginia deserved everything the judge pronounced, and more.

"First, he pronounced a three-week sentence behind bars."

"No!"

Now why would Noelle, who owned a king-sized headache, given the hour she spent unconscious, and the size of the bruise on her chin, feel a moment's distress over her attacker's sentence?

"'Til I reminded the judge that meant I had to tend the prisoner, something I didn't want to do."

"Oh." Noelle seemed a mite pleased.

"She can't get off scot-free."

Noelle thought that over. "No, I suppose not."

"Her daddy's mad as a wet hen."

Noelle's pleasure widened into a grin. Somehow, when he wasn't paying attention, she'd come closer, her little hand landing on his forearm and squeezing.

How he wished he could slam the door on his newfound awareness of Noelle as a woman.

"Come, sit. I must hear this story."

He grabbed the excuse to extricate himself, and took the closest chair at the big kitchen table. "The bread smells mighty good, ma'am."

She already had a knife in hand, and sliced thick pieces. Sliding two onto plates, she offered both. He gladly took the heel, and reached for the butter crock and honey she set on the table.

Over the afternoon repast, they laughed over Mayor Abbott's antics, the argument he debated before the circuit judge, and the judge's determination that Miss Abbott would be tried for her actions, despite her parentage.

Noelle's laughter washed over him, absolution for his foolishness.

He'd laughed that night. Laughed like he hadn't in ages. He found himself smiling now, fairly basking in this woman's kindness.

He wouldn't allow anything further.

In time, this... *awareness*... would pass.

"She loves you, you know."

He swallowed his last bite of bread and licked a drop of honey from his finger. "Naw."

"Yes. She told us all she'll wed you, and the house that she grew up in will be hers once more."

He'd wondered about that. "That's crazy talk— not you, Noelle. *Virginia.* Those stories are all her own."

"Then why did she do it?"

He shrugged. "Blame it on the full moon. Brings out the crazy in some folks."

Reviews Matter!

One link makes it wicked **easy to review** this short story, no matter where you purchased it.

One Quick Click:
www.KristinHolt.com/one-quick-click-the-witching-eve

Thank you for reading *The Witching Eve*, my first published *short story*. I hope you found it enjoyable.

This story falls between two previously published titles, **MAYBE THIS CHRISTMAS** and **THE MARSHAL'S SURRENDER**. Both titles tell Gus's story; the first brings him to Mountain Home, Colorado in search of Effie, and the second, heals his heart and allows him to risk a new beginning with Noelle Finlay. If you've not yet read one or both of these titles, you'll find they're currently enrolled in the **Kindle Unlimited program**, making them available, without additional charge, to readers subscribed to that affordable monthly service.

I love the process of researching elements of history in order to set a fictional tale against an accurate historical backdrop. As I typically do, I want to share a little bit about the history—what is accurate, and what I finessed to make it work—within this short story. At the back of kindle editions, I ensure this section has links allowing readers to click through and discover the historical background. Working with the limitations of paperback books, I've provided a page on my website with all of this content. It's super easy to find:

www.KristinHolt.com/History-Witching-Eve
(don't worry about the capital or lower case letters, but the spelling is critical; remember Kristin is "e-free").

In truth, the full moons in October (8th) and November 6th), 1900, missed All Hallow's Eve. I couldn't resist taking artistic license and moving the full moon to Halloween. Historically, the "recognized truth" that "Lunar Lunacy"—acute madness associated with the full moon—was well known. Folks believed everything from sleep quality to fertility (and onset of childbirth pains) to criminal behavior. Twenty-first century science has disproved all such claims.

The traditional practice of fortune telling, including baking small representative objects into a cake, is accurate to history. These are merely two of dozens of games played by the youth in an attempt to foresee their future events (including identity of spouse), quality of marital life, and financial status.

Victorians adored ghost stories. Halloween was far from the only occasion for telling spooky tales. Dickens and his famous ***A Christmas Carol*** is a fine example. Ghost stories were often part of at-home parlor entertainment for families or when entertaining guests.

The practice of playing pranks on neighbors (and blaming witches) was widespread in the United States in the 19th century. Numerous newspaper articles illustrate the types of pranks played, the tolerance of such as "all in good fun", and the prevalence of such behavior. "Trick-or-Treating" is a twentieth century development, and first occurred several decades into the century. The Victorian Era (1837 to 1901) was imbued with hand-me-down rituals from the Old World (every nationality of immigrants brought their beliefs and traditions with them). Halloween was mostly brought to the United States by Irish and Scottish immigrants during the 19th century, and was gradually assimilated into mainstream American society.

You'll find *The Jolly Halloween Book* (referenced before short story), published in 1900, on **Forgotten Books**, **Amazon**, **Free Ebooks**, and more.

Most of my recent titles have their own Pinterest board. **Come see the images that inspired various elements of this story**, including the little things baked into the "Halloween Cake"...

Remember, you'll find links to much more of the history and detailed information at this easy link:

www.KristinHolt.com/History-Witching-Eve

My warmest thanks for reading *The Witching Eve*. I hope you found both the story and a peek at the historical setting of this novella to be enjoyable. You're invited to visit my website page for the *Holidays in Mountain Home* series [**http://www.kristinholt.com/holidays-in-mountain-home-series**] to explore other titles in this loosely related series (where each title stands alone). As this instance shows, not all "holiday" books are about Christmas.

With warmest appreciation,

Kristin

P.S. to find my page:

www.kristinholt.com/holidays-in-mountain-home-series

more quickly, see:

http://bit.ly/2A754ZY

(case sensitive)

or scan this code:

HOLIDAYS IN MOUNTAIN HOME *Series*

In Chronological Order:

Courting Miss Cartwright (Rocky & Felicity), **1879**
Book 5, Founder's Day NOVELLA

This Noelle (Phil & Caroline), **1881**
Prequel: Book 0.5, Christmas NOVELLA

The Gunsmith's Bride (Morgan & Elizabeth), **1885**
Book 6, Independence Day NOVELLA

Unmistakably Yours (Hank & Jane, Oscar & Ina), **1887**
Book 8, Thanksgiving NOVEL

Home for Christmas (Hunter & Miranda), **1898**
Book 1, Christmas NOVELLA

Maybe This Christmas (Luke & Effie), **1899**
Book 2, Christmas NOVELLA

The Witching Eve (Gus & Noelle), **1900**
Title 7, Halloween SHORT STORY

The Marshal's Surrender (Gus & Noelle), **1900**
Book 3, Christmas NOVEL

The Drifter's Proposal (Malloy & Adaline), **1900**
Book 4, Christmas NOVELLA

http://www.kristinholt.com/holidays-in-mountain-home-series